Sit Sip Nap

Written by Caroline Green
Illustrated by Begoña Corbalan

Collins

tip it

tip tip

pat it

tap tap

sit in

sit sit

sip it

sip sip

nap in it

nap nap

tip tip tip

it tips

14

After reading

Letters and Sounds: Phase 2
Word count: 26
Focus phonemes: /s/ /a/ /t/ /p/ /i/ /n/
Curriculum links: Understanding the world
Early learning goals: Reading: use phonic knowledge to decode regular words and read them aloud accurately

Developing fluency

- Your child may enjoy hearing you read the book.
- Read the text together, having fun with the repeated words, such as **tip tip**, and reading them with expression, e.g. **nap nap** on page 11 could be read sleepily.

Phonic practice

- Point to and say the word **nap** on page 10. Ask your child if they can sound out each of the letter sounds, then blend them. (n/a/p – **nap**)
- Turn to pages 12 and 13 and repeat for **tip** and **tips**. (t/i/p – **tip**; t/i/p/s – **tips**)
- Look at the "I spy sounds" pages (14 and 15). Point to and sound out the /n/ at the top of page 14, then point to the woman's face and say "naps", emphasising the /n/ sound. Point to the man on the television and say: man – listen for the /n/ sound in man. Ask your child to name other things in the picture which contain the /n/ sound. (e.g. *nut, nutcracker, nose, newspaper, nest, newsreader, nine, necklace, knitting needles, window, handle*)

Extending vocabulary

- Turn to pages 2 and 3. Ask your child:
  o Where do you think the woman is? (*in her kitchen*)
  o How many things can you name that are in her kitchen?
  o Can you name more things that are in your own kitchen?